To the brothers

BRIDGET
and the
Moose Brothers

Pija Lindenbaum

Translated by Kjersti Board

R&S
BOOKS

Stockholm   New York   London   Adelaide   Toronto

Bridget's room is too quiet,
and she's tired of it.
She wants a brother or a sister,
a small, thin one
that will fit in her doll's bed.
Or else a big brother
who plays loud and noisy music.

Her closet and her drawers
contain only Bridget's things.
No big-brother shoes
and no tiny diapers.

BRIDGET

Then Nicky arrives.
He is going sledding on
his saucer
in back of the building.
Bridget also wants to
go sledding,
with a terrific swoosh
down the hill!

"My saucer will go fifteen or eighteen miles per hour," Bridget says.
"Mine will go a THOUSAND!" says Nicky.

When they get to the hill,
all of Nicky's brothers and sisters are there,
and some kids that Bridget doesn't know.
"Check out the jump they've made!" Nicky shouts.
"There's an awful lot of people here," Bridget says.
She really wants to go sledding with Nicky, just the
two of them.

Bridget suddenly realizes that she's cold.
She thinks she had better go home.

But in front of the entrance to her building
some moose are sitting, blocking the way.
They, too, are tired of sledding on saucers.
"Let's go to my place instead," says Bridget. "You can
be my brothers! At my place, we're allowed to play
with balls inside. And we have lots of soft rugs."
"Sounds good," the brothers say, and clip-clop into
the elevator.

"Let's do it again!" they say when the elevator stops
at the fourth floor.
"The elevator is not a plaything," says Bridget. "Here
we are now!"

Bridget shows them the way to her room.
"This is where I live!" she says.
"But first, wipe your feet."
Then she puts the brothers in the middle
of all her Lego pieces.

The brothers fool around a bit.
Then they sit down, right on the Legos.
The brothers don't know what to do.
They're not used to this.

"I'm going to draw," says Bridget. "Who wants to join me?"

Bridget hands out some paper.
Her drawing is very clever: a pink bird with blue tights.
The brothers draw mostly thunderstorms and knives.
"Oh, that's nice!" Bridget says, even though she notices
that they are breaking almost all of her crayons.
She collects the stubs.
In any case, the brothers don't have the patience for drawing.

"Hey, this looks like my cousin!" says one of the brothers,
finding a zebra under the rug.

"Let's play with the animals instead," Bridget suggests.
She arranges them very neatly, as if they were in a zoo.
The zebra mother belongs with her children.
The elephant family goes by the water trough.
But that's not the way the brothers play.
They throw the crocodile up in the air.
And the lion eats all the monkeys.
"Yippee, here comes Spiderman!" one of the brothers calls out,
and hurls the penguin across the room.
It lands way up on a shelf with a clinking sound.

That's where Bridget keeps her most treasured things,
including a porcelain Sandman with glitter along the edge
and a taxi that's really, really old.
"Don't worry!" the brothers shout. "We'll get it."
"It doesn't matter," Bridget says quickly.
"Leave it there. I'll show you where you'll sleep instead."

She pats the thick, soft rug with her hand
and goes off to find some pillows and a comforter.

But there's no need, for the brothers have
already settled down in Bridget's bed.
"This will be great!" they say.
"Come to think of it—we only sleep in huts."
"Oh," says Bridget. "I don't have any huts.
Don't you think it's time for some juice now?"

"No. We have to fix something," the brothers answer,
for they have found a better place to sleep.
"Then we have to check to see what's on TV."

Bridget picks up a dress and drapes it over the edge of the bed.
"I thought you needed a little sister," she says.
"Someone who really loved you.
This is not the way it's supposed to be. Is it?"

But there's no answer, and when Bridget turns around,
the brothers are not there.

They're in the bathroom
getting a drink of water from the toilet.
Disgusting!
"I'll give you water in a glass instead," says Bridget,
and puts the toilet lid down.
"No way!" the brothers answer,
galloping out of the bathroom.

"Hey, we want some popcorn!"
the brothers shout from the sofa.
They have turned on the TV even though
it isn't time for Sesame Street yet.
"You can't have any," says Bridget.
"Besides, you're not allowed to eat popcorn
on the sofa."
"Are you allowed to JUMP on the sofa?"
the brothers say, laughing.
"Are you allowed to stand on your antlers?"
"ARE YOU ALLOWED TO LIE DOWN IN THE
BUTTER?" they bellow.

Bridget realizes that she no longer wants any
brothers. They make too much noise.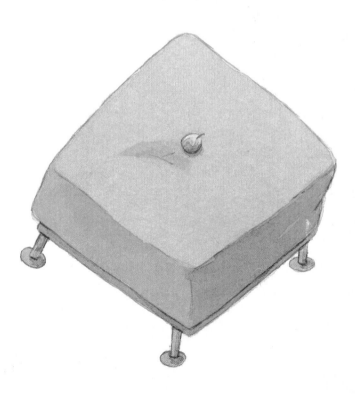
"This is all wrong," she says. "You had better
play outside."
"No, we're not done with the hut," they shout.
"But moose are SUPPOSED to be outside," Bridget says.
"Playing hockey?" they ask.
"If they want," Bridget answers.
"No way!" the brothers say.
"Well, we can ride the elevator," Bridget says.
"Several times! Is that cool, or what?"

They would love to do that.
They ride the elevator, down and up,
up and down,
until the brothers have had enough
and their stomachs begin to hurt.

When Bridget pushes the door open,
the brothers tumble outside into the snow
and start to wrestle.
"You were a nice little sister!" they call out.
"But when all is said and done, we prefer to
be outside in the cold."

Then they turn and wave
before scampering off.

Bridget's room is nice and quiet.
Bridget scoops up all the moose poop and throws
it away.

I have Nicky, she thinks, and the kids at day care.
I don't need any brothers.
Then tonight my cousins are sleeping over.
And Hedda's very good at drawing horses!

The End

Rabén & Sjögren Bokförlag, Stockholm
www.raben.se

Translation copyright © 2004 by Rabén & Sjögren Bokförlag
All rights reserved
Originally published in Sweden by Rabén & Sjögren under the title
GITTAN OCH ÄLGBRORSORNA
Copyright © 2003 by Pija Lindenbaum
Library of Congress Control Number: 2003107755
Printed in Italy
First American edition, 2004
ISBN 91-29-66046-7

Rabén & Sjögren Bokförlag is part of
P. A. Norstedt & Söner Publishing Group, established in 1823